Albert and the Apple

Dr Arin

Introduction

ALBERT

ALBERT'S MOTHER

ALBERT'S GRANDMOTHER

One summer afternoon, Albert had nothing to do. He played with his friends all day and had his nap too.

He went to the kitchen and found his mother peeling some apples on the counter.

4

7

OK, I choose these ones. I will look for a place to plant them. I will be right back mother!

He walked around the house, but could not find space to plant his seeds, So he walked to grandma's home, 6 houses away from his.

When he reached her house she was creating embroidery for a blanket. It looked like a tiny blue mouse.

Albert planted the seeds and visited them every morning.

He watered them daily without fail.

The plants started sprouting and growing into big apple trees. Albert proudly says that these are all his.

As the years passed, the seeds grew into 2 trees. Then another one grew, then there were 3.

You were right, mother. Planting seeds was worth it. Now I have trees, many apples, many seeds. Can you imagine how many people each apple tree feeds?

Let's say each tree had 10 red apples that sold for a pound each. You would earn 10 pounds per tree.

More trees, more apples, and you could earn many 10 pound notes. With more apples, you're most likely to become rich!

21

Draw your favourite characters

23

Draw your favourite characters

24

Draw your favourite characters

25

Draw your favourite characters

26

Draw your favourite characters

27

Draw your favourite characters

28

Draw your favourite characters

29

Draw your favourite characters

Acknowledgements

Thank you to the
AVIVA foundation
for their support
with this project.

Thanks to the
bMoneyWize team:
Agatha, Grace,
Dani, Wunmi, Polde,
Laura and Richard.

Albert and the Apples tells a simple story for pre-teens who are learning about money. Albert has a new idea to help his mum who is cooking with apples. He intends to grow some apples to help his mum.
He decides to search for good ground to plant his apple seeds. To his surprise, after taking good care of his plants, they grow into trees. There are now so many apples that Albert can sell.

This book is designed to appeal to children through the use of bright colours and humour. It teaches children about hard work and investing for a good return.

Learning about money should be fun and relatable for everyone, including children.

Lightning Source UK Ltd.
Milton Keynes UK
UKHW050734090223
416597UK00009B/243